# Dark Star

Written by Melanie Joyce
Illustrated by Anthony Williams

## Titles in Full Flight Girl Power

Badger Publishing Limited
Oldmedow Road, Hardwick Industrial Estate,
King's Lynn PE30 4JJ
Telephone: 01438 791037
www.badgerlearning.co.uk

2 4 6 8 10 9 7 5 3

Dark Star      ISBN 978 1 84691 034 0

First edition © 2006
This second edition © 2013

Text © Melanie Joyce  2006
Complete work  © Badger Publishing Limited 2006

Series Editor: Jonny Zucker
Publisher: David Jamieson
Commissioning Editor: Carrie Lewis
Editor: Paul Martin
Design: Fiona Grant
Illustration: Anthony Williams

# Dark Star

## Contents

# The Letter

Tyler woke suddenly. The dream was fresh in her mind. She could still hear that voice: "Return the key."

Why did she feel so afraid? It was only a silly dream.

Tyler reached under her pillow and pulled out a star-shaped object. It was solid silver.

Holding it made her think of Gran. She had given it to Tyler for her seventh birthday. It always made her feel better. Tyler smiled. Then she remembered. How could she have forgotten? Today was her 13th birthday.

Downstairs there were presents. Then Mum handed Tyler a letter.

"It's from your gran," said Dad. "She wrote it before she died, but asked us to keep it until today."

Tyler opened the letter.

> *My darling Tyler, it is time for you to know who you really are. The Earth is in danger. Evil powers will soon have taken it over completely. Now you are 13, it is your task to stop them. The silver star I gave to you is very special. It is a star key. Go to the old stones at Castle Tor tonight. Put the key on the altar stone. Altea will help. Tell no one. Hurry my darling. There is little time.*
>
> *Gran*

Tyler read the letter again. She thought of the dream. Did someone want the star key? Who was Altea? What would happen at the stone circle?

It was time to find out.

# Shadowlands

Early that evening Tyler left the house. She took her rucksack and a map. It was two hundred miles to the stone circle. She could get the train. But what about her parents? They would know she was missing. Tyler had to think of something.

She texted Sash.
**Can you cover for me tonight?**

The phone beeped in reply.
**Got a hot date?**

Tyler laughed. "Trust Sash!" She walked down the hill. It wasn't far to the station now.

Tyler didn't see the two figures who followed her. She crossed the road.

The phone beeped. It must be Sash again. Only it wasn't.

**WE KNOW.**

Tyler froze. She looked around. There were lots of people. Was someone watching her?

Across the street stood a woman. She was tall and dressed in black. Beside her was a small man. They stared without moving. Tyler felt uneasy. The woman raised her hand. The phone beeped again.

**GIVE IT TO US.**

Tyler knew she had to run. She raced past the station, down the hill and into town. Saturday shoppers filled the high street. She pushed through the crowds. In panic she looked back.

The tall woman was following. Where could she run to?

At the corner, Tyler looked behind again. Suddenly she tripped and fell. Hands grabbed at her. She tried to get up. But there was no escape.

"It's alright, it's alright," said a voice. "I'm Altea."

Tyler looked up at the woman. Red hair and large green eyes. A face you could trust.

"Come on," said Altea, "this way."

The pair fled down an alley. It led to a car park at the back of the shops. Soon they were at Altea's car. Safely inside they locked the doors.

"I'm sorry I frightened you," said Altea. "I had to make sure you were safe. The Evil Powers know who you are. They want to stop you. We have to set the key in the stone at sunrise."

Tyler started to calm down. "Two people were following me," she said. "They knew my mobile number."

"They are runners," replied Altea. "Ordinary people who are controlled by the Power. They have no idea what they are doing. Only you can help them."

Tyler was silent. She felt scared. Then the message came.

**DON'T RUN.**

Altea switched on the engine and drove off. Tyres screeched as the pair sped away. They headed for the motorway.

The sun was sinking in the sky. Soon it would be dark. It was going to be a long night.

# Impact

As they headed north the weather changed. It began to rain. Drops hit the windscreen. The roads became narrow and dark. There were no streetlights. Outside it was pitch black. Now and then fox eyes shone in the headlights. Tyler and Altea had been driving for hours.

Tyler was exhausted. There had been no more text messages. Maybe they were safe? Before long Tyler fell asleep.

Then the dream came. The voice was louder now. It seemed to be coming closer. Tyler's phone beeped and she woke suddenly.

**WE'RE COMING.**

"Oh, no," said Tyler.

"What?" asked Altea.

Suddenly a horn blasted. Headlights flashed. Someone was behind them. They were getting closer, trying to overtake. A big four-wheel drive was right behind them. The windows were blacked out.

"It's them!" cried Tyler.

"Hold on!" said Altea. But it was too late. The tyres skidded and the car spun off the wet road. There was a loud crunch of metal. They had landed in a huge ditch.

Altea was stuck. "It's my leg," she groaned, "I think it's trapped."

Tyler leaned over to help. "Come on," she said. "I'll get you out."

But Altea put her hand up.
"Tyler, you've got to keep going," she said. "Find the stones. Set the key."

Tyler hated to leave. But there was no other way. She had to reach the stones before sunrise.

# Lost and Found

Tyler climbed out of the car. She looked around. Which way would the stones be? It was so dark. She took a moment to think. The star key was in her pocket. It felt cool and smooth.

Tyler suddenly felt stronger. She went up to the top of the bank. Her feet slid in the mud, but the key seemed to pull her forwards. She walked into the darkness, but there were sharp dips and rocks in her way.

Tyler tripped and fell. She dropped the key and felt around in the grass for it. But there was no light. It was useless. What was she going to do? Without the key all was lost. Tyler was sure she had failed.

Just then something glinted. There it was again. Tyler went carefully towards it. She reached down. A bright shape lay in the grass. It was the star key.

Then there was a noise. Tyler looked up.

A few metres in front of her was a huge stone circle. How had she not seen it before? There were thirteen giant stones. The largest stone was at the centre. Tyler made her way into the circle. There didn't seem to be anyone around.

At the centre, the huge altar stone lay on its side. At one end there was a star-shaped hole.

"It's just like the star key," thought Tyler. She knew what to do. Pulling the key from her pocket she started to put it into the stone.

In the shadows, something moved.

# Light and Dark

"Stop," said a voice.

Tyler froze. A figure stepped out from behind a stone. It was the woman who had been following her. She looked pale and her eyes were blank.

Beside her stood the small man. The woman took a few steps forwards. She reached out her hand. When she spoke, her voice was dull.

"Give it to me," she said.

Tyler knew what the woman meant.

But she had come too far to give up now. "If you want it, come and get it," she said.

The woman raised her hand higher. Tyler felt as if something was pressing down on her. She tried to cry out but she could not move. The Power pushed her down. Tyler fell to her knees. She dropped the key.

The man stepped forward. He moved like a robot. Tyler could see his eyes were blank too. It was as if he was sleepwalking. The man took the key. He stepped back towards the woman.

Tyler was powerless. She could not move. There was no way out of this. Had she really failed this time?

Suddenly there was a scream. The man fell forward. The star key dropped to the ground. Behind him, Altea came limping into the circle. Over the hill, the sun was beginning to rise.

# The Power

The pale woman turned. She fixed her
angry eyes on Altea. As she did, Tyler
was released from her grip.

"Get the key," screamed Altea.

Tyler leapt forward. She grabbed the
key.

Altea fought with the woman. It was
hard to hold her. "Hurry!" she cried.

Tyler had to act quickly. She ran towards the big stone. With shaking hands she set the key in the star-shaped hole. It fitted like a glove. Tyler turned the key.

Everything seemed to stop. A silence fell. Then a soft hum started. It grew louder. Tyler could feel it in her feet. Soon the hum was a roar. It seemed to shake the stones. The pale woman held her ears. She sank to her knees. "Stop!" she wailed.

The small man looked blank. Outside the circle, Altea lay still. Was she dead?

Tyler could not move. It was like being in a dream. On the altar stone the key was lit up. Then it moved around the circle. The stones began to glow. Tyler closed her eyes. Light was all around her. It lit up her body. Suddenly her eyes snapped open.

Tyler had the Power. She knew what to do.

# Endings and Beginnings

Tyler walked slowly towards the woman. She reached down and took the woman's head in her hands. Dull eyes stared upwards. Tyler looked deep into them. She wanted the woman to be well. A look of fear flashed across the face. Then it passed. The woman's body fell limp. But she was not dead.

After a while she opened her eyes. "Where am I?" she said. "Who are you?"

"I'll explain later," said Tyler. She went to help the man. Soon he was awake too. Like the woman, he remembered nothing.

At the edge of the circle, Altea staggered to her feet.

Behind her, the sun rose in the sky.
The darkness was gone. A new day
had begun.

"Come on," said Altea. "It's time to go home."

Tyler thought of home. It meant good things. Seeing Mum and Dad. Going to school. Hanging out with her friends. All the things that were normal. But nothing would ever be normal again. Because now Tyler knew who she really was. This adventure might have ended. But really it was just the beginning…